City Boy

by
Alan Combes

Illustrated by Aleksandar Sotirovski

Dedicated to the memory of Mike Vernon

With special thanks to:

William Asbridge
Charlie Barnes
Charlie Bil
Euan Courtney
Ryan Fitch
Bailey Gray
Amelia Isom
Amber Jeskins
Samantha John

Kai Johnson
Henry Lay
Adam McGilton
Sebastian Newman
Harley Restrick
Jay Santiago
Sophie Silsby
Callum Wootton

First published in 2011 in Great Britain by
Barrington Stoke Ltd
18 Walker St, Edinburgh, EH3 7LP

www.barringtonstoke.co.uk

ISBN: 978-1-84299-489-4

Printed in China by Leo

Contents

Chapter 1
Football Crazy

Josh Grant was football-mad. He lived out in the country with his mum, his sister Abby, and Suzy the black and white collie dog. His granddad lived with them too, in a tiny flat above the garage.

Josh's granddad Ron had been a footballer many years ago. He had helped

Sheldon City to win the title for two years running and he kept the medals from those days in a frame next to his door.

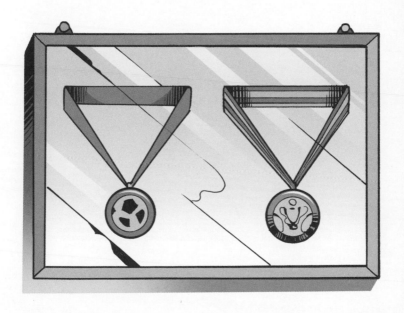

"Why do you keep them there, Granddad?" Josh asked him once.

"So that every time I go out, I remember the best days of my life," his granddad said.

Granddad Ron also had a loser's medal from the FA Cup Final. He kept that one in a secret place and only showed it to one or two people.

"If there is one regret I have about all the great times I had in football," he told Josh, "it's losing the Cup Final."

He told Josh how Sheldon had been winning the Final 1–0 with just 10 minutes to go. Granddad Ron had made a bad mistake and put the ball in his own goal to make it 1–1. Big Billy Brown, the Spurs striker, had headed the winner with 10 seconds left to play.

There were tears in Granddad Ron's eyes whenever he told this story.

It was Granddad Ron who helped Josh to become a footballer. They always watched *Match of the Day* on the TV together. Josh asked his granddad lots of questions about the game.

"What made George Best such a good dribbler?" he asked.

"Because he was a two-footed player. He could use his left foot as well as his right," Granddad said.

"Wayne Rooney has the hardest shot I've ever seen, Granddad. Could you hit a ball that hard?"

"No, but I was a defender, not a forward," Granddad said.

Josh learned how to play the game with his granddad's help. Granddad was lame now so he couldn't kick the ball, but he could tell Josh what to do.

Josh was right-footed, so when he was kicking a ball round the yard, his granddad only let him wear a boot on his left foot.

"Ow, it hurts when I kick it with my right foot," Josh moaned.

"Good! It was meant to," Granddad said. "Now you need to use the left foot."

Suzy the dog tried to pinch the ball off Josh as he dribbled. It was fun, but it made Josh cross at times.

Slowly Josh became a two-footed player.
Granddad made him study a DVD of George
Best. "The greatest footballer ever,"
Granddad said. Then Granddad set up a
dust-bin and made Josh shoot at it from the
other side of the yard.

"You have to knock it over to score a goal," he told Josh. "Just hitting it doesn't count."

Josh knocked it over two times in his first five shots. His mum came out and told them off about all the noise they were making.

"You scored!" Granddad said softly when Mum had gone back indoors. "Eat your heart out, Wayne Rooney!"

In the game called "Keepy-up", Josh had to keep the ball in the air using his feet and his head.

"If you can do it 50 times without the ball hitting the ground, you get a pound. For 100, I'll give you two pounds," Granddad said.

His granddad spent a lot of money as Josh got better at keeping up the ball.

Chapter 2
Five a Side

Josh's family didn't have much money.
His mum had a job two days a week as a
secretary in a sports club. On those days,
Granddad was in charge, but most of the
time Josh and his sister were at school. At
weekends, the children helped with the
house work.

Josh never played matches for the school team. He lived too far away. Even on a Saturday morning, he couldn't get to school to play because his mum didn't have a car.

In PE lessons, Mr Simms the teacher told him what a good player he was.

"We could do with you in the school team," he said.

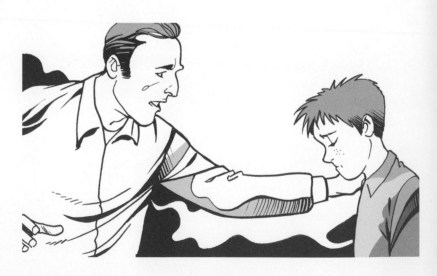

"Sorry, sir," Josh said. "I have to help Mum at home."

A new teacher, Miss Cutts, arrived at school. To everyone's surprise, she started a five-a-side lunch-time league. Josh's mate Mark Scott told him about it.

"A lady teacher doing football?" Josh asked, puzzled.

"She's in one of the top ladies' teams," Mark told him. "She plays for Wales."

"Wow!" was all Josh could say.

At home he told his granddad about it.

Granddad was excited. "Sign up for a team, Josh. This is your chance."

The lunch-time league games were a great success. 10 teams signed up and Josh joined with his mates Mark Scott, Tom Bull, Andy Shaw and Will Jones in a team they called Pirate Raiders.

Their first game was against Crazy Cats. Josh was amazing. He could dribble and shoot and control the ball better than any other player. By half-time Josh's team were winning 2–0 so Crazy Cats brought on a sub named Pete Ross.

Ross was a hard player, and his job was to stop Josh at any cost. Every time Josh tried to dribble past him, Ross would tap his ankles or give him a hidden kick. The ref never saw a thing.

"Pass to me, Josh," Tom yelled. But Josh shot instead.

"Give me it now, the goal's empty," Jack shouted, but Josh tried to dribble past everyone.

In the end, Josh's team lost 2–3.

In the dressing room, it was silent. No one spoke to Josh.

"We all lost," Josh said. "Why are you blaming me?" He was black and blue all over, thanks to Pete Ross getting at him all the time.

At last, Mark spoke up. "We're dropping you for the next game, Josh."

"Me? Why? I scored both our goals," Josh said, about to cry.

"You're ball greedy," Will told him.

"So what if Rossy was fouling you?" Tom added. "You could have passed the ball to one of us."

"Yeah, learn how to pass," Jack said.

In his lessons that afternoon, Josh felt sad. What his team said was true. Granddad had taught him many skills, but not how to pass the ball.

Chapter 3
Passing

Granddad could see something was wrong when Josh got home.

Josh came into the house from the school bus, threw his bag onto a chair and got a drink from the fridge. Then he sat at the table, staring out of the window.

"What about starting on your homework?" his mum said.

"Or chopping up that wood for the fire?" Granddad asked.

Josh got up. He was angry. "Why can't people just leave me alone?" he yelled, going up to his bedroom.

After 10 minutes Granddad came into Josh's bedroom.

"What's wrong?" he said. "Was it the five-a-side?"

Josh told him about the game. "I scored two then it all went wrong."

"How did it go wrong?" Granddad asked.

"They said I was greedy. I didn't pass the ball."

"Hmm," said Granddad, "that's a problem. We live so far out of town, we have no one to practise passing the ball to."

Suddenly Granddad cheered up. "I think I've got an idea. Fetch Suzy."

Suzy the dog was a quick learner and soon Granddad had her running round the yard in a big circle.

"Don't kick the ball hard," Granddad said.
"Just fire it at Suzy as she runs round you."

"Why?" Josh asked.

"The trick is to put the ball in front of
her as she runs."

Each time Josh did that, Suzy would dribble the ball back to him using her nose. Then she would run in a circle again.

"This will help you to be a good passer of the ball," Granddad said.

That night, as the family sat eating their meal, Josh's mum looked upset. She picked at the food on her plate.

"What's the matter, Mum?" Josh's sister, Abby, asked.

Mum turned to Abby. "We are short of money," she said. "The rent has gone up and so have bus fares and everything else."

Josh began to panic. "Can you get a better job, Mum?"

"I've tried but it's not easy," his mum said. "I'm sorry but I think we'll have to move to a smaller house."

Josh and his sister were very upset. Leave the house they had grown up in? Things just couldn't get any worse. Or so it seemed.

Chapter 4
The Big Day

The next week started well. The Pirate Raiders players changed their minds and let Josh play in their lunch time game. They won 4–0 and Josh had an excellent game.

Mr Simms, the PE teacher, was watching. He phoned Josh's mum. "Can Josh play for the school against Hall Street this Saturday?" Mr Simms asked.

"I can't get him there. We don't have a car and there's no bus," Josh's mum said.

"The school will pay for a taxi," Mr Simms said. So Mum said he could go and Josh was thrilled.

Granddad saw him off in the taxi on the Saturday morning. "Lots of passing the ball," he reminded Josh.

After 20 minutes of the game they were 1–0 down.

At half-time, Mr Simms moved Josh to the middle of the pitch.

"Plenty of passes to the wingers," he told Josh.

It worked a treat and by full-time Josh's school had won 3–1. Josh didn't score, but everyone agreed he was man of the match. Even hard man Pete Ross shook his hand and told him he had been amazing.

But when the taxi pulled up by the gate at home, Josh knew something was wrong.

The house was silent. Suzy wasn't running around and his mum had no washing on the line.

He walked in the back door and saw his mum and sister sitting silent at the table.

"What's the matter?" he asked. "Where's Granddad?"

"Sit down, Josh," his mum said. "Something bad has happened."

Josh sat down.

"I'm sorry, Josh, but Granddad Ron is dead. He died in his chair, about an hour after you left. We didn't have any way to call you."

At first Josh held back the tears. Then he went up to his bedroom. He lay down on the bed and cried until his mum knocked on the door and went in.

"Granddad always said that if anything happened to him, you had to have these," his mum said, and put the two league medals on the pillow beside Josh.

"I don't ever want to play football again," Josh said, between sobs.

"Stop that," his mum said. "Granddad was my father and I will miss him a lot, but he trusted you, Josh. He knew you could make it. Don't let him down."

Granddad's funeral was a very sad day. Some very famous old footballers were there.

"A great player and a great man, was Ron," Josh heard Bobby Charlton say to his mum.

When they got home from the funeral, a letter was waiting for them. Josh's mum looked very upset after she read it.

"This is it, Josh and Abby," she said. "I was trying to find a way for us to stay here. But the bank won't help. We'll have to leave the house."

Josh and his sister looked at one another across the kitchen table. They had been sad all day. Now they were sad and afraid.

Chapter 5
A New Start

Two weeks later, Josh came down to breakfast to find his mum looking the happiest she had been for ages. In her hand she held a letter that had come in the post that morning.

"Josh," she said, "which is your favourite football team?"

"You know it's Sheldon City," Josh said. Granddad had been their coach after he stopped playing.

"Would you rather watch Sheldon City play than Man United or Arsenal?"

"Of course I would," Josh said. "I'm a big fan. Everyone at school knows I'm a City boy!"

"Well," Josh's mum said, standing up, "you're looking at Sheldon City's new office secretary!"

Josh snatched the letter from his mum and read it.

"Wow, Mum! Why didn't you tell me?"

His mum told him she'd kept the job a secret till she knew for sure so Josh and Abby didn't get their hopes up.

"Does that mean we can still live here?" Abby asked.

"It would be too far for me to travel," Mum said. "Plus, a house in Sheldon comes with the job!"

Josh had to leave his old school, which made Mr Simms, the PE teacher, sad.

"We could have won the league with you, Josh," he told him on his last day.

Josh went to a much bigger school, Sheldon High. Most days, after school, he took Suzy to Sheldon City's training pitch and did passing practice. Granddad would have been pleased about that. It was floodlit after dark in winter.

Just before Christmas, some boys from the Sheldon City junior squad saw Josh playing with Suzy and the ball. They were 4 years older than Josh but it didn't stop them.

"Good skills," one of the boys told Josh. "I'm impressed. How did you learn them?"

Josh didn't want to tell any one about Granddad.

"The dog taught me," he joked, and the players fell about laughing.

The juniors told their coach, Jack Hunt, about Josh. One night Jack hid in the stands with them and watched Josh train.

The next day he spoke to Josh's mum in the office.

"Is that your boy who turns up with his dog each night for training?"

"It is. He loves his football," she said.

"I'd like him to play for City Juniors," Jack Hunt said. "He's good."

"Well, he already has two league title medals," Josh's mum said.

Hunt was puzzled.

"They were his granddad's!" Josh's mum laughed. "Ron Grant was my dad."

Chapter 6
What Happened Next

The rest is history.

Josh Grant went on to become the youngest ever player in an FA Cup Final.

He didn't play from the kick off. The manager sent him on as a sub when the score was 1–1 with 10 minutes to play. He was just 17 years 34 days old, and the City fans were shocked when he ran on to the pitch.

He came on because Peter N'Grondo, the South African winger, was hurt.

Because no one knew Josh, Rovers did not bother to mark him properly. The ball ran loose to him after a mix-up in the goal mouth. Josh blasted it past the Rovers' keeper. His granddad would have been proud of the way he kicked it. City were 2–1 up. Seconds later the ref blew for time and the fans went wild.

City had won the cup and Josh had got a winner's medal.

"This one's for you, Granddad," he shouted as he ran round the pitch on his victory lap.

After that Josh played in City's first team most of the time. Soon he was called up for England.

Thanks to Granddad Ron, Josh could shoot, dribble and juggle the ball. But Josh's best skill was his passing. He had Suzy the dog to thank for that.

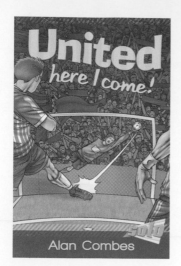

United Here I Come!
by
Alan Combes

Joey and Jimmy are very bad at football. But Jimmy is sure he will play for United one day. Is Jimmy crazy – or will he get there?

The Night Runner
by
Alan Combes

Greg wants to win the race. Every night he trains in secret on the school field.
But he sees a spooky shape in the moon-light. What is it? Should he run for his life?

Bomb!
by
Jim Eldridge

The clock is ticking ...
Rob's a top bomb disposal
expert. He has to defuse
a bomb in a school before
it's too late.
Can he do it?

I Spy
by
Andrew Newbound

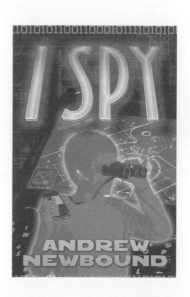

Finn borrows his spy dad's
top secret work gear to
become 'School Spy'.
When Tom gets bullied,
he calls on Finn to help
him out. Can Finn and
Tom beat the bullies
together?

You can order these books directly from our website at
www.barringtonstoke.co.uk